Barney's Sing-along
If You're Happy and You Know It!

Adapted from the traditional
by Dena Neusner
Illustrated by Darren McKee

SCHOLASTIC INC.

New York   Toronto   London   Auckland   Sydney
Mexico City   New Delhi   Hong Kong   Buenos Aires

If you're happy and you know it,
clap your hands.

If you're happy and you know it,
clap your hands.

If you're happy and you know it,
then your face will surely show it.

If you're happy and you know it,
clap your hands.

If you're happy and you know it,
stomp your feet.

If you're happy and you know it,
stomp your feet.

If you're happy and you know it,
then your face will surely show it.

If you're happy and you know it,
stomp your feet.

If you're happy and you know it,
jump up and down.

If you're happy and you know it,
jump up and down.

If you're happy and you know it,
then your face will surely show it.
If you're happy and you know it,
jump up and down.

If you're happy and you know it, dance around.

If you're happy and you know it, dance around.

If you're happy and you know it,
then your face will surely show it.
If you're happy and you know it,
dance around.

If you're happy and you know it,
shout **HOORAY!**
If you're happy and you know it,
shout **HOORAY!**

If you're happy and you know it,
then your face will surely show it.

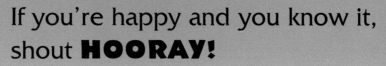

If you're happy and you know it,
shout **HOORAY!**

If you're happy and you know it,

clap your hands,

stomp your feet,

jump up and down,

dance around,

and shout **HOORAY!**